AURADON PREP

Power of Good

Born to Rule

Be Yourself

AURADON PREP

Born to Rule

Be Yourself

Power of Good

Spirit Book

Highlights & Memories

White Plains, New York • Montréal, Québec • Bath, United Kingdom

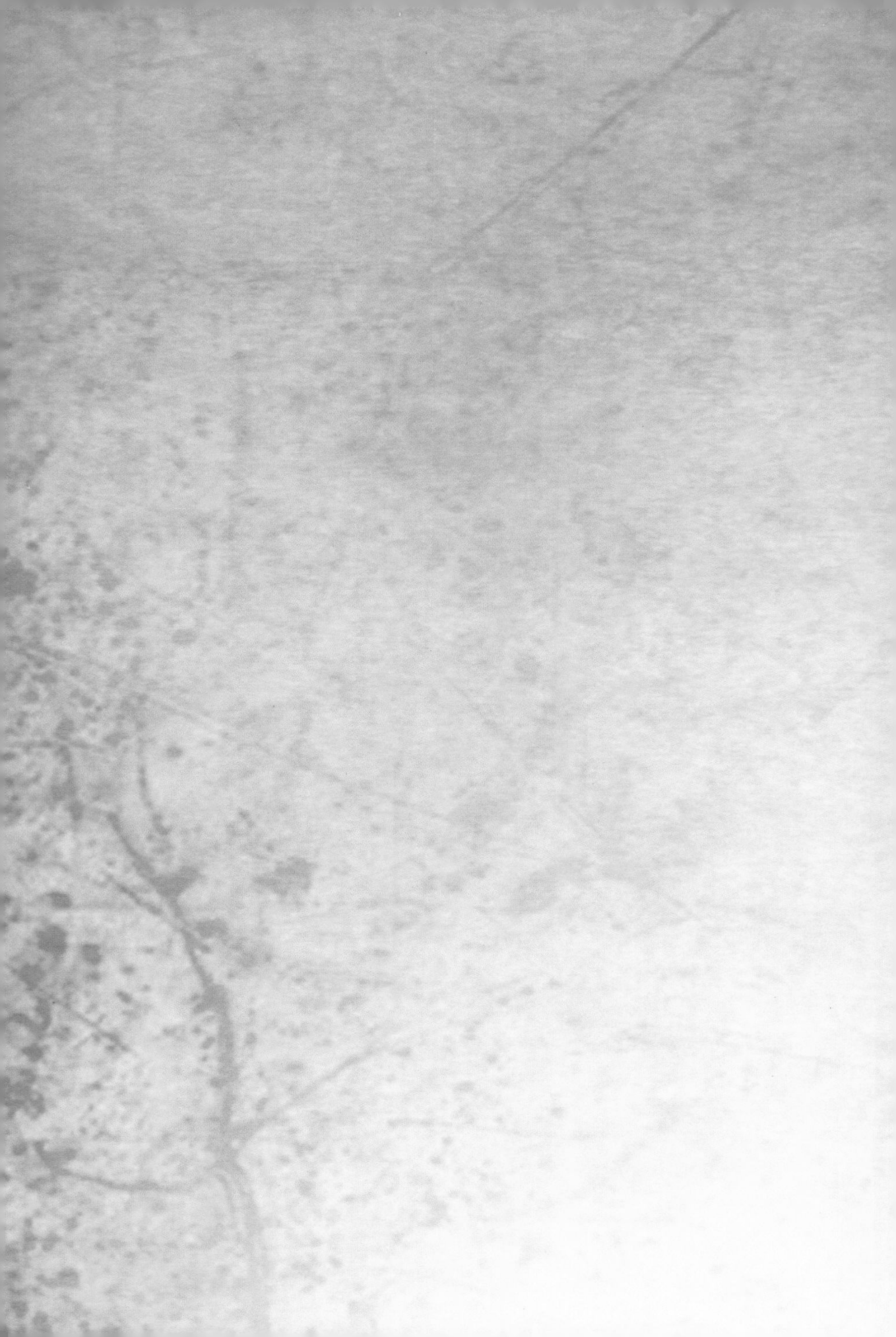

AURADON

Do children bear the responsibility for the misdeeds of their parents? I don't believe that...

I believe in redemption and forgiveness of our enemies, which is why I brought four exchange students from the Isle of the Lost to join us at Auradon Prep this year.

After looking over several potential candidates, I narrowed down my choices and decided on four kids of some of the most infamous villains in history.

These are the worst of the worst:
Jay—son of Jafar
Evie—daughter of the Evil Queen
Carlos—son of Cruella de Vil
Mal—daughter of Maleficent

My coronation is right around the corner, and as heir to the throne of Auradon I need to show everyone I'm ready to make tough decisions.

Dad always tells me, "A good king stands by his decisions." So whether for good or for bad, I'm taking a bold stand on this issue.

I truly believe these kids can prove themselves to be good—all they need is the same opportunity my friends and I had being born to heroic parents—and not villains. I know I won't be the same ruler as my father, so maybe these kids won't follow in their parents' footsteps, either.

We'll never know unless we give them a chance. To me, it's worth taking the risk.

—Ben

Welcoming plan for
the Isle of the Lost Kids to
Auradon Prep:

- SMILE! Make them feel welcome.
- Be friendly—even if they're not.
- Give a tour of the campus and point out ALL the fun historical details.
- Direct everyone to the correct dorm rooms, so they don't get lost.

Or steal anything!
—Audrey

Doug's always the friendliest guy around campus.
—Lonnie

Wow—look at her.
What else can I say?—Doug

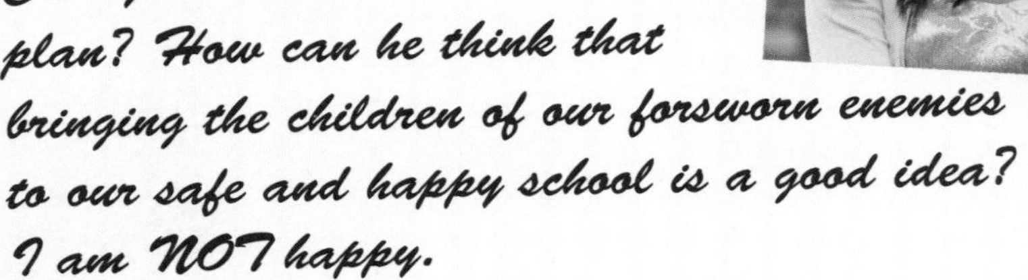

The Apple Doesn't Fall Far from the Tree

Can you believe Ben's outrageous plan? How can he think that bringing the children of our forsworn enemies to our safe and happy school is a good idea? I am NOT happy.

My friends and entire family live in Auradon. And now we're letting these VILLAINS into our midst and expecting them to be good! The sons and daughters of the Evil Queen, Jafar, Cruella de Vil—and Maleficent?

MAL-E-FI-CENT—as in, the evil sorceress who almost destroyed my family! Well, I'm not buying it!

Ben may be naive enough to believe in second chances. But I KNOW that the poison apple doesn't fall far from the tree.

—Audrey

See? Stealing! —Audrey
What is wrong with that guy? —Chad
Not sure I like what's going on here ...—Audrey

Family Honor

I'm super excited to have four kids from the Isle of the Lost joining us at Auradon Prep this year. While I think it's a fantastic idea and could really help these kids find their inner goodness, lots of you still have reservations.

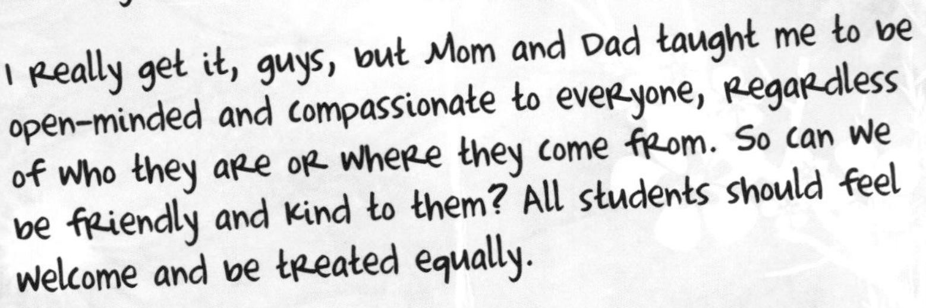

I really get it, guys, but Mom and Dad taught me to be open-minded and compassionate to everyone, regardless of who they are or where they come from. So can we be friendly and kind to them? All students should feel welcome and be treated equally.

It's a matter of Fa family honor. —Lonnie

Looks like a tough crowd...this may not be so easy.

Remind me to never mess with Lonnie...
–Evie

Lonnie wouldn't hurt a fly!
—Jane

Why I Love Tourney

Life must be pretty sweet for the reigning MVP of Auradon Prep's Fighting Knights. Oh, wait—IT IS, because I am the reigning MVP of the Fighting Knights! Last year, I really held the Tourney team together and pushed harder than any other player to take us to victory.

It's not the team's fault I'm so good at this sport. When you're good, you're good. I love Tourney more than anything. Someday, I may go pro. Until then, they better start polishing another plaque with my name on it for the school trophy case—I have no intention of giving up my Tourney title anytime soon.

—Chad

Look at these clowns! I knew this was a bad idea. At least they won't be challenging my MVP status. –Chad

Don't be so sure about that!—Jane

Who's the clown? —Carlos

No Honor Among Thieves

Stealing has always been a fact of life for me—I take what I need and get what I want. I look out for ME, and that's the way I like it. Dad sent me out to find choice items: weapons, trinkets, watches, heirlooms—anything to make a profit at Jafar's Junk Shop. There were even times when we sold some idiot's stuff back to him! No honor among thieves, as they say.

Now that these Auradon nerds have let Mal, Evie, Carlos, and me come to Auradon Prep, I'm drooling from all the fine swag to lift: gold, crowns, jewels...these rich kids are LOADED! Hard to believe they're letting us walk around without so much as a metal detector! Can't wait to see the looks on their faces when they realize they've been robbed blind. —Jay

French Fries? Seriously?!—Mal

The best stuff I've ever stolen from the worst of the worst:

- Dr. Facilier's voodoo doll
- Gaston's crossbow
- Cruella's emerald ring
- Captain Hook's backup hook

Dad sent this to us the first week of school.
—Jay

'm SO
mbarrassed!
—Evie

You can't choose
your family... —Mal

You can say that again.
—Carlos

Growing Up

You might think being the daughter of the Mistress of All Evil is easy—but it's not! I try to make Mom proud, but I worry about living up to her expectations.

I've tried talking to Evie, but she doesn't get it. Her mom only cares about being pretty (ugh) and eliminating the competition (as if).

My mom expects the very worst from me—every single day! I don't know how she does it. Committing endless heinous acts is exhausting!

If she only knew I AM doing the worst I can.

It just never seems bad enough!
She's always saying things like:

- I saw you steal gold from that shop—
  but you didn't break anything on
  your way out!
- Nice name-calling...but they
  should've been crying by the time you were done!
- When you graffiti something, you have to make
  it BIGGER than that! (And in a better spot.)

I do have a leg up on this whole evil thing.
I'm the daughter of the greatest villain
ever known. My family connection alone
is enough to strike fear into the hearts
of every lowlife on the Isle of the Lost.

If there's one thing I know—
I'm rotten to the core.

You can do this, Mal!

Sugar and Spice and Everything Nice

There are such high expectations growing up the daughter of Fairy Godmother. Everyone expects me to be good...ALL. THE. TIME. I try my best to not disappoint—but it seems the other students avoid me because of it.

Maybe if I was as athletic as Lonnie, or a princess, like Audrey, people would pay attention to me. Or if Mom allowed me to use magic once in awhile instead of just studying it, I definitely would be more popular. No one wants to be friends with plain Jane—let alone the headmistress' daughter. I have to think of something BIG this year to get noticed.

—Jane

Fairy Godmother's Rules for Good Spirits

1. Look on the bright side of life—negativity is not allowed.

2. Always wear a smile and share it with the world.

3. Magic is for making other's dreams come true, never for personal gain.

I use spells for my own gain—all the time. —Mal

You're no Fairy Godsister, sister! —Audrey

4. Work on the inside, not the outside—true beauty lies within.

Outer beauty never hurts, though.-Evie

As long as you love yourself for who you are, there's nothing wrong with either! —Lonnie

But high school's not so black and white. —carlos

True—I'm learning to balance the rules with a dose of reality. —Jane

Fear the Furry

Jay says I complain about my mother, Cruella de Vil—like, A LOT! But what does he expect from the son of one of the most selfish, most high-maintenance, most demanding women alive?

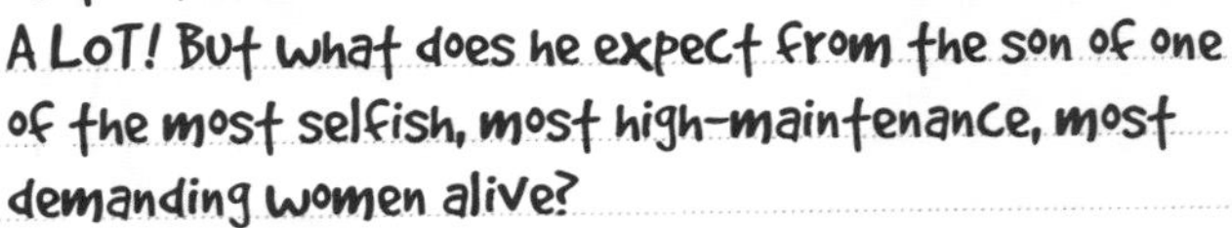

I've had to do so many awful chores for her! Ten times a month I had to scrub the grime off her roadster—I think she drives through mud puddles on purpose just to make sure it's nice and dirty. I hate digging through her mothball-smelling wardrobe and laying out her garish outfit for the day. And don't even get me started on picking the clumps of gloppy hair out of her hairbrush.

I have wanted to stand up for myself for so long. But Mom says if I ever stop being her evil boy, they'll come after me...the DOGS! As scared as I am of her, dogs scare me even more! They're nothing but vicious, drooling, bloodthirsty predators that will attack you as soon as they see you...at least, that's what Mom tells me. I must figure out some way to stand up to my mother.

—Carlos

UPDATE:
Mom gave me a list of "Dog Facts" that just aren't true.
For instance, here are some true facts:

- Dogs cannot paralyze you if you look them in the eye.
- Dogs can't breathe fire (so it's okay to wear hairspray around them).
- A dog's bark won't permanently deafen you. (Good-bye earplugs!)
- Dogs eat dog food and treats—but not boys.
- Dog slobber isn't acidic and can't melt through steel.

—Carlos

That's totally messed up! —Audrey

I'm glad we could clear these things up for you, Carlos. —Ben

Things I Like About Dude

I have to get my hands on that mirror! –Chad
You are so charming...
I think. –Evie
Awkward!
—Mal

Evie totally has a thing for me. And why wouldn't she? I am the most handsome, most eligible, most CHARMING guy at school, after all! Turns out she's got this magic mirror that reveals the answer to ANY question. In other words—it's the perfect way to cheat my way through school.

Mom and Dad promised to throw a party for me if I got good grades this year. Now all I have to do is lead Evie along and convince her to do my homework... and there's a chance I'll get it. Wait—maybe I'm both charming AND a genius!

—Chad

Mirror, mirror, on the wall,
who's the fairest of them all? Nobody ever asks magic mirrors who's the smartest of them all or who knows the square root of 4,105.73378 (it's 64.076)... When you're the Evil Queen's daughter, nobody's really interested in what you have to offer besides your looks. Mom always said that I didn't have to be smart because I was pretty. That's all guys are interested in, right?

Lately, I feel like I have so much more to offer. I'm actually really smart! I've never seriously dated before—it's SUPER fun just to flirt. But what I really want is someone who can hold a conversation, who cares about what I say and not just about how I look. Do I have to play dumb to get noticed? Shouldn't my potential Prince Charming be interested in the real me?

Someday my prince might come—but what if Mom's right? A Mr. Perfect who is interested in my beauty AND brains might not exist. I might have to settle!

—Evie

Princely Crushes

Who's a girl gonna crush on? Decisions, decisions... -Evie

Chad is so hot! —Audrey

Well, he is pretty-(pretty dim). -Evie

I would never DREAM of stealing my bestie's BF (even if he is insanely cute)! Girl code! -Evie

Smart.
Funny.
Sweet.
He's such a big geek, though!
-Evie

love a guy with some brains!
—Lonnie

Plus, he's a really talented musician. —Jane

Go for it, Evie! —Mal

Auradon Prep is unlike any other school around because you learn not only academics, but also what it takes to be a good leader:

- Honesty: You're only as trusted as your word!
- Positivity: Maintain a sunny attitude through stormy weather.
- Responsibility: Accept your triumphs AND failures.
- Determination: Never give up!
- Confidence: Believe in your strengths and in the strengths of others.
- Decisiveness: Make the tough choices.
- Loyalty: Commit to your causes, principles, and friendships.
- Empathy: Walk a mile in someone else's shoes.
- Knowledge: Inform your decisions with intelligence and wisdom.
- Inspiration: Inspire goodness in others and be inspired to better yourself in return.

—Ben

Leadership sounds like a LOT of pressure! —Jane

Helping the children of today
[be]come the heroes and heroines of tomorrow.

Here's a look at my coronation program. —Ben

I don't think I could ever be a king.—carlos

I should say not—you're just a peasant. —Chad

You don't have to be Royalty to be a leader, Chad! —Lonnie

Be the Reflection You Want to See

Today is the day I reach out to the kids from the Isle of the Lost. They don't seem really all that bad. Mal even used her magic to fix up Jane's hair. It looked so cool...I'd love for Mal to do MY hair!

It's time to let my reflection be the change I want to see in the world. My friendship might help the others get over their preconceived notions about Mal, Evie, Jay, and Carlos. I don't think they're anything to fear. I just have to take the first step.

—Lonnie

I just love my new hair!
—Lonnie

Late-Night Snacks

A late-night snack with good friends. —Lonnie

But why does everyone look so distressed? —Lonnie

I can attest—love potion aside, they tasted delicious. —Ben

There's nothing a nighttime heart-to-heart and cookies can't fix! —Mal

What about split ends? -Evie

Mirror, Mirror...

My compact is an actual shard from Mom's Magic Mirror. It can't speak anymore but it's still incredibly powerful. —Evie

My Magic Mirror always tells the truth and is super helpful for finding anything. Lost your favorite hairbrush? No problemo. Can't find the answer to a tricky test question while studying? It can help find the answer to that, too! —Evie

Can it help us find boyfriends? —Lonnie

Wasn't the Evil Queen's Magic Mirror evil?
—Audrey

Magic is neither good nor evil—it's all about who's using it. —Jane

Mom and I have always loved our mirrors.–Evie
Can't believe Mom let me take this with me! –Evie
Here I am trying it out for the first time. –Evie

As head cheerleader, it's up to me to get Auradon Prep's cheer squad rooting for the Fighting Knights and entertaining the crowd! —Audrey

The Fighting Knights couldn't score without the support of our cheer team! –Chad

Speak for yourself, Charming. —Jay

We're #1! –Chad

GO, Fighting Knights! —Audrey

Looks fun! Maybe I can add some hip-hop flair! —Lonnie

I'd sooner be caught in knock-off heels!
-Evie

True Spirit Means Looking Your Best!

With the right dress and some gold accessories, you'll feel like royalty in no time. —Audrey

I never knew someone could rock "cotton candy" chic. (Too swee for my tastes.) —Mal

Let me make you something with a little BITE!
-Evie

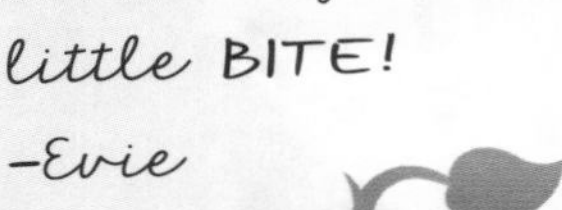

You don't need magic sleep to be beautiful. But a full night's rest does wonders for your skin. —Audrey

If anyone knows the importance of the right makeup techniques to bring out your fairest features, it's my mother. –Evie

- Always start with an oil-free foundation that matches your natural skin tone.
- I use pronounced eyeliner with subtle eye shadow to make these beautiful browns sparkle.
- Shape your eyebrows to follow their natural shape.
- Try different lipsticks to find what looks good on you.
- A little bit of blush goes a long way to bring out those cheekbones.

When applying makeup, remember the best thing Mom ever taught me-always use upward strokes!

There's a lot of magic in Auradon—
but to me, music IS the best magic.
Melodies combine into songs, pluck at our
heartstrings, and beat like a drum on our
souls. To me, there's nothing else like that
in the world! Music can excite people, it can
inspire them, it can make them fall in LOVE.
Tell me, how is music any different than
magic?

—Doug

Wish I could charm her
away from Chad.

Some might think I'm a nerd for liking school—but I wouldn't trade these classes for a mountain of gold!
—Doug

Doug's a genius when it comes to chem. –Evie

It's what everything's made of!
—Doug

Seriously... one of you has to tutor me or Mom won't let me play Tourney. –Chad

Rocks and jewels have always fascinated me. I love spending my summers down in a mine with Dad and my uncles digging out glittering gemstones! —Doug

Must be a geologist thing.
–Chad

Seems like dirty work! —Jane

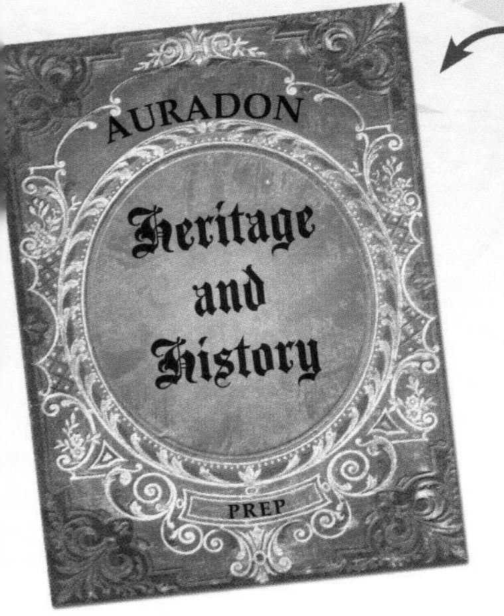

A class devoted to telling our parents' stories and the stories that came before them. —Doug

And remembering that we're NOT our parents. —Jay

We are all free to make our own stories.—Ben

I think that's the most important lesson of all.
—Mal

The Best BF
all of Aurado
—Audrey

The "Best BF in
Auradon" broke up with
you for me.
—Mal

UGH! It's not enough that those Isle of the Lostians are becoming more popular—that Mal has stolen Ben! Well, Chad's WAY better than Ben, anyway!

How is no one else seeing how awful they are? They're not here to learn. They're not here to make friends. What are they playing at? I know those no-goodniks are up to something...I just don't know what. I can't stand it...everyone else may be buying their act—but not ME.

—Audrey

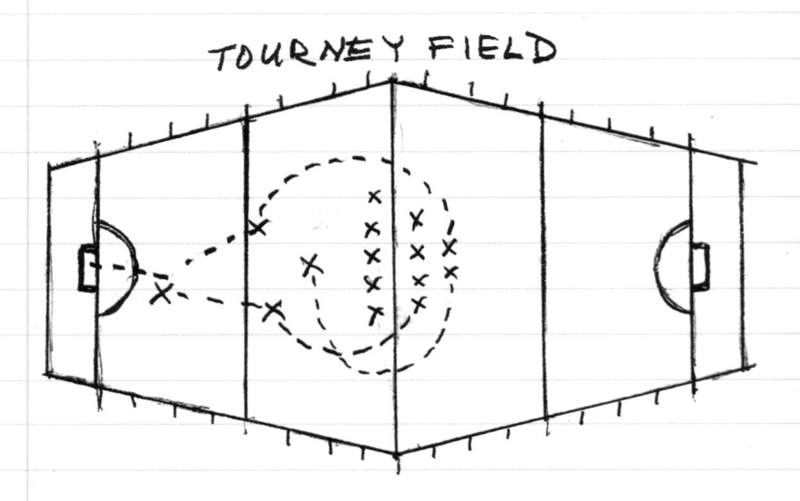

Tourney is Auradon's favorite pastime. Basically, two teams battle to hit the game ball into the Kill Zone. Using sticks, you carry, pass, and shoot the ball—NO HANDS ALLOWED. Players on defense use shields to stop the other team from moving down the field, while manned blasters on the sidelines fire projectiles to take out a player.

—Chad

Whatever, Charming!
I play by my own rules!
—Jay

Playing video games
is way better.
—carlos

Fighting Knights won finals! —Ben

Those Sherwood Falcons don't know what hit them. -Chad

We've got SPIRIT!
Yes, we do!
We have SCHOOL SPIRIT
how 'bout you?
—Lonnie

Chad's #1! —Audrey

More like runner-up #1!
This year's MVP is ME!
—Jay

School spirits? I might have a spell to banish those.
—Mal

I picked turf from my teeth for weeks, but Tourney is the GREATEST!
—Carlos

I'll stick with band, thanks.
—Doug

You did great, Carlos! —Jane

Thanks for being such a great team captain, Ben! —Jay

Thanks for not letting me get squished, team! —Carlos

We wouldn't let our Most Improved Player get hurt, Carlos! —Ben

Tourney

My new favorite sport! —Jay

You are a great addition to our team, Jay! —Ben

Jay tackles like a runaway horse and carriage. I would know! —Chad

'cause you spent most of Jay's first practice flat on your back! —Carlos

Totally can't believe I found something I'm good at here—Tourney! Coach Jenkins said I have natural physicality and athleticism, which apparently makes me perfect for this sport.

I never understood teamwork until now. Dad used to say, "There's no 'team' in 'I,'" but Coach explained it in a way that makes sense to me. If the body is a team, then each part is a player—the head makes the plan, the legs run the field, the arms catch the ball...and I'm the FIST. I hit hard to make sure the rest of the body can do its job. I kinda like that.

In a way, Mal, Evie, Carlos, and I are a team, too. Each of us helps and supports one another, even though we make fun of each other sometimes or have our own ideas. We stick together because we're not just partners-in-crime—we're family.

This is some heavy stuff to think over. I'm so used to looking out for myself I never thought teamwork could accomplish so much more!

—Jay

Graffiti and Artwork
BargainCastle

Mal's artwork was graffitied all over the Isle of the Lost. —Carlos

She was kind of a big thing back home. -Evie

I'm STILL a big thing! —Mal

These are really neat, Mal. I wish I was artistic. —Jane

Anyone can make art—it's all about self- expression. —Mal

Don't Underestimate Me

I can't believe I ever thought pretending to be dumb would make guys like me. I never focused on intelligence. With my mother, everything was always vanity... beauty... power. That's not what I want anymore. I love learning—and now I'm not afraid to show it, thanks to encouragement from a special cutie pie.

I'm pretty AND smart—a dangerous combination for anyone who underestimates me because of my looks. Auradon Prep better watch out! Evie's coming back with more confidence, more understanding, and a fierce new attitude! I've surprised even myself with just how far I can go. -Evie

Picnic by the Lake

The Enchanted Lake in the Forest of Eden. THE best spot for a romantic date. —Mal

Chad's surprising me with a candlelight dinner there next week. —Audrey

I wish a guy would take
on a romantic date to the
Enchanted Lake. —Jan

I am? –Chad

Don't worry, Audrey, I'll help him throw something together. –Lonnie

We don't have these back home. My new all-time favorite food! —Mal

These crystals form in the Enchanted Lake because of the purity of the waters. —Mal

I have to get one—it'd make a fierce necklace!–Evie

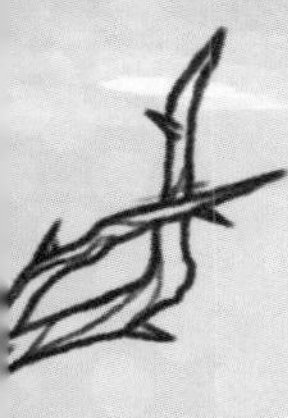

Couldn't ask for better company. —Ben

I always imagined I'd fall for a nice girl, but Evie's unlike anyone I've ever met before. She's fun and smart—and even though she puts on a tough-girl facade, deep down I think she's a good person. I never thought someone as beautiful as she is would ever go for someone like me—let alone the fact that I never thought I'd have to convince my dad, six uncles, and Auntie Snow White to let me date the daughter of their worst enemy!

—Doug

The Fairest of Them All —Doug

Does Doug actually have a crush on Evie? —Mal

He won't stand a chance! —Carlos

She'd tear him apart! —Jay

Guys, give me a little credit! —Evie

Never knew Doug was such a romantic! —Ben

He put in little checkboxes and everything! —Lonnie

GUUUUUUUYS!!! —Doug

Evie, I'm so proud of you for studying hard and using your head to get good grades! I'd love to see you away from the textbooks sometime. Would you be up for that?

☐ Yes ☐ Maybe ☐ No

Always yours,
Doug

Auradon Prep offers so many awesome classes, it's hard to decide which is the best! Here are two of my favorites! –Evie

Remedial Goodness

At first I thought it was lame! Now I appreciate everything I learned on becoming the best person I can be. –Evie

I had a hard time in this class... —Jay

You kept stealing Fairy Godmother's Chalk! —Carlos

Chemistry

One of my favorite subjects at Auradon—not surprising, considering Mom's penchant for brewing up potions! —Evie

Mom taught me that love's a pretty big component in lifting enchantments. —Jane

What's the formula? Lithium + Oxygen + Vanadium + Erbium? —Doug

Love doesn't have a formula—it's its own element! —Evie

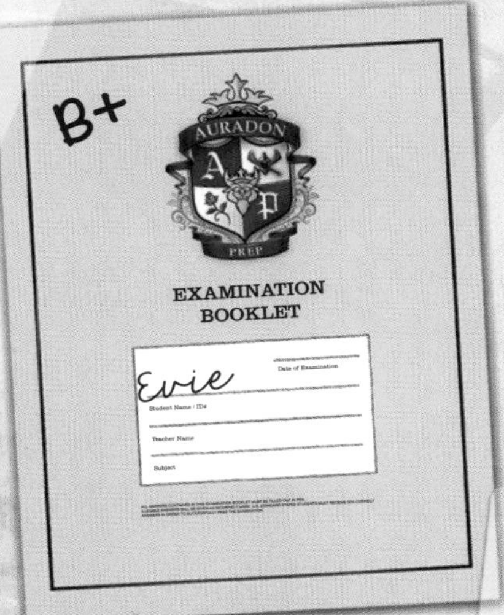

First test I ever got a B+ on! Thanks to hard work and study—and no Magic Mirror. —Evie

Way to go, Evie! Really impressive. —Ben

Our Favorite Video Games

The single greatest invention EVER! —Carlos

Go-Go Ballroom Dancing

You've been invited to a grand ballroom and must show off your dance moves by matching your own movements to what's shown on screen. —Carlos

I always beat you at this one!
—Jay

You cheat by tying my shoelaces together! —Carlos

Carriage Crush

A racing game where you control a horse and carriage trying to get your passenger to an awesome party and home again before midnight. —Carlos

Why does that sound familiar?
–Chad

Really, Chad? –Evie

Storm the castle

As a heroic prince, you have to avoid enemies and traps as you climb higher and higher up the forbidden fortress until you defeat an evil dragon to save the princess. —carlos

I'd rather be the dragon stopping the prince. —Mal

It'd feel weird to be the evil boss instead of the hero. —Lonnie

What about a princess saving the prince from the dragon? —Audrey

An old philosopher said that dance is the movement of the soul. —Lonnie

Guess he never saw Carlos dance! —Jay

Hey! I dance like no one's watching. —Carlos

No one IS watching. It's rude to stare. Haha! —Mal

I love to dance with a guy across a ballroom. SO romantic. -Evie

I'm too shy to ask a boy to dance. —Jane

Let the boys come to you, Jane! —Audrey

Best bros!

Carlos is like a cool little brother to me. —Jay

We play games together...

It's so cute how you boys fight. —Evie

We fight over stuff...

That's an understatement. —Mal

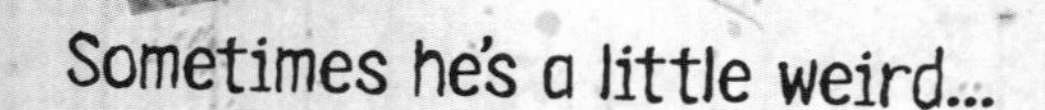

To be fair, I was TERRIFIED of dogs when this was taken. —Carlos

Who's afraid of dogs? —Jane

The son of Cruella de Vil...the whole Dalmatian thing? —Ben

Oh! That makes sense. —Jane

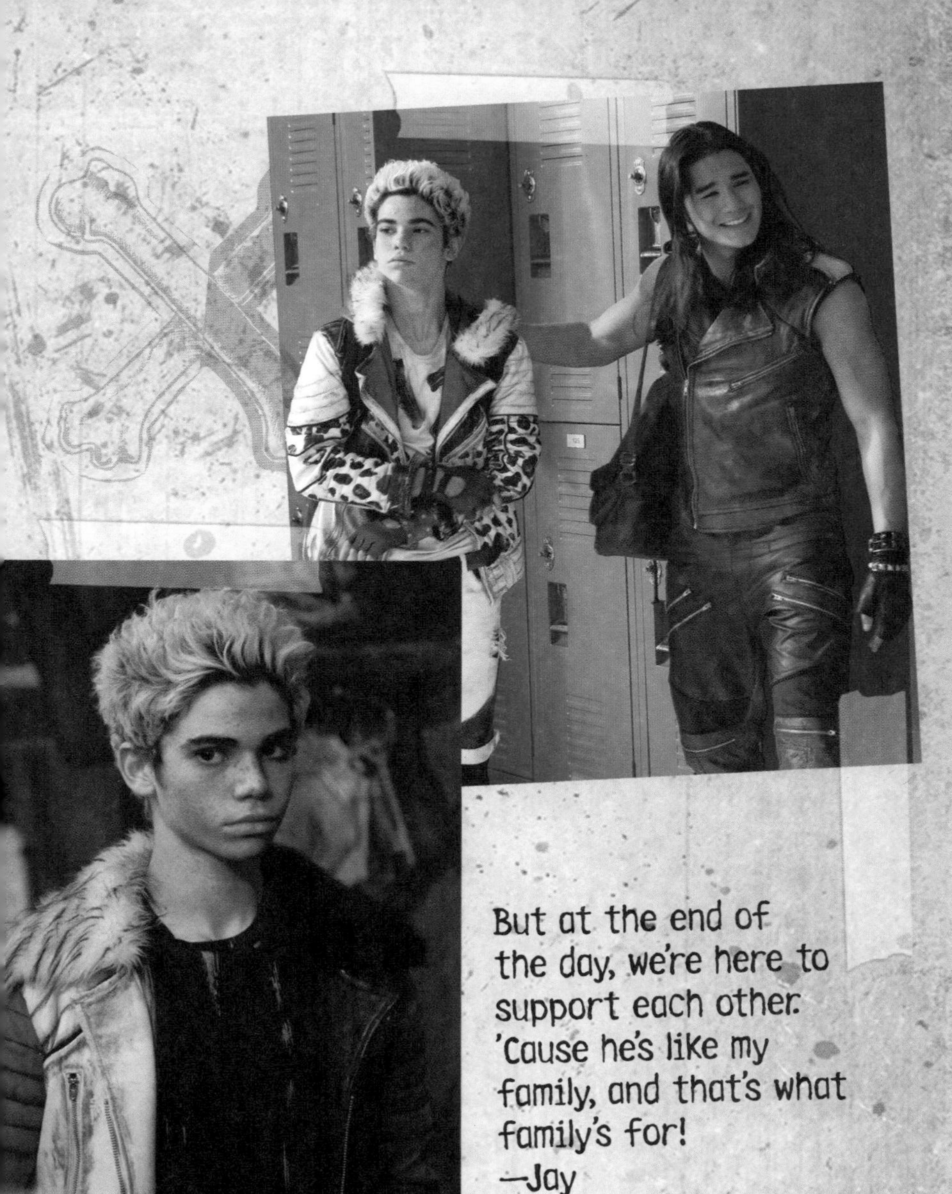

But at the end of the day, we're here to support each other. 'Cause he's like my family, and that's what family's for!
—Jay

That's supes adorbs!
—Audrey

KING ~~Prince~~ Ben

Prince Chad

Being royalty makes you better than anyone else.
—Chad

That is wrong on SO many levels, Chad.
—Mal

Hey! Where's my picture on this page?!
—Evie

Seriously the BEST girlfriend at Auradon Prep!
—Chad

Royalty

Princess Audrey

You two deserve each other.—Evie

I truly wish you both every happiness.
—Ben

Gorgeous Princess snags perfect Prince—Happily Never after! —Audrey

Bibbidi-Bobbidi Mom!

My mom always encourages others to find the best within themselves—magic or not.
—Jane

Where would I be without Fairy Godmother?
–Chad

Her daughter's pretty cool, too! —Mal

Aww...thanks, Mal! —Jane

Mama's Boy No More

I DID IT!

I finally stood up to Mom, and it felt amazing inside! My entire life she's been bullying me into doing every nasty little thing she could think of—but now I know she was just using me like her trained lapdog so that she didn't have to do anything herself.

It's been such an incredible year: I got over my fear of dogs, I made a lot of new friends, I found out I actually like being good—and best of all, I learned more about myself than Mom ever gave me credit for.

Coming to Auradon with Mal, Evie, and Jay has been life-changing. And it's just the beginning! Now that I'm away from my mom, I don't have to be afraid of stuff all the time. With Dude and my friends by my side, I'm totally looking forward to what the future has in store for us.

—Carlos

Spells + Magic

Oops! Caught in the act.
—Mal

Contains every spell and charm
a girl could need! —Mal

A Spell for Better Hair

Beware, forswear,
Replace the old
with new hair.

Pretty Inside and Out

All I've ever really, really wanted was for people to accept me—it's the biggest wish I've ever wished! I was never the "pretty girl" like Audrey or Lonnie, but Mom insisted I focus on my "inner beauty." What good is that, when no one notices you?

That's changed, now! Earlier this year, Mal went out of her way to encourage me to come out of my shell, and suddenly everyone wanted to be my friend! She even used MAGIC to give me a new hairstyle (which everyone loved). And it's all thanks to the kindness of a villain kid. Maybe they're all not so bad....

It's really confusing, but I know one thing for sure—I like how I'm feeling, both inside and OUT!

—Jane

So many new friends! Thank you, guys, for being there for me! —Jane

I already considered you a friend, Jane—but I'm glad we've grown closer. —Lonnie

It's definitely been a year to remember. —Doug

I came here with three friends. Now I have TONS! -Evie

For Ben's coronation, I wanted Mal's and my dresses to be completely out-of-this-world rocking! So I went for a full-length look with flowing, richer fabric textures and brighter colors than I'm used to, but the results speak for themselves. –Evie

- Large collars are making a comeback! Grab some attention and stand out from the crowd.

- A tiara or jeweled comb will complete the outfit to make anyone feel like a princess.

My Signature Style

- Royal blues (obvi) and ebony blacks, with a hint of apple reds.
- A crown accentuates my natural hairline while adding some pop to my locks.
- This capelet hints at my royal heritage and gives some natural flow to the outfit.
- An industrial skirt and platform boots add some sass to my strut.

Evie ALWAYS looks amazing.
—Doug

Always work the perf accessory—mine is a bright red heart pendant.—Evie

Using Magic for the First Time

I am SO embarrassed by my behavior at Ben's coronation. I screwed up big time. Thankfully, everyone's been pretty cool (except for Mom, who grounded me BIG TIME).

Biggest lesson? My actions can have serious consequences—especially if I don't think them through. I never realized how much concentration goes into harnessing magic. From here on out, I will try doubly hard to focus on my studies.

Despite the consequences, using real magic for the first time was exhilarating!

—Jane

Sorry for being so judgmental! —Chad

You guys Rock! This year was just the beginning of the amazingness! —Lonnie

My first royal proclamation as King of Auradon: I hereby decree that the reformed villains known as Mal, Evie, Jay, and Carlos be absolved of any and all past wrongdoings during their first year at Auradon Prep. In the end, they all chose GOOD—which is to be commended, not punished.

Furthermore, I encourage all of us to examine our own shortcomings as heroes and heroines. Remember that no one is perfect. Because of this, it is our duty as loyal citizens of Auradon to try our hardest to be our best selves—even kings.

Signed,

H.R.M. King Ben of Auradon

To err is human; to forgive, divine. —Doug

We're really sorry for all the trouble, guys. —Evie

And promise to do better next year! —Jay

We'll make it up to everyone, we promise! —Mal

You guys are the best things to happen to Auradon Prep! —Jane

Thanks for not giving up on us. —Carlos

PARDONED

Okay, so maybe I wasn't the best person I could've been this year. What sucks more is that everyone really likes those Isle of the Lost kids now. I'm still stoked that we won the championship, but that Jay needs to be knocked down a peg or two next year!

Watch out, Jay—I'm gunning to retake MY MVP spot!

—Chad

Maybe I was a little harsh on Evie, Jay, Carlos...even Mal. But I was right about their plotting something. Can't blame a girl for protecting family and friends, right?

Still can't believe those guys would ever choose good over evil. Mal and the others are here to stay—whether I like it or not. Maybe next year I can try to be nicer to them all...just a bit. Thanks for saving us!

—Audrey

Friendship isn't weak or ridiculous. It's actually really amazing.

Friendship Is the Most Powerful Magic

When I first came to Auradon, I never imagined where I would end up. I finally stood up to Mom and made tons of new friends—and my boyfriend is now King! How crazy is THAT?!

But through everything, I learned that real magic doesn't come from wands or staffs or spellbooks. It comes from friendship. And friendship is the most powerful magic of all.

Friendship transformed me from the inside out—from a wild child who truly believed all she wanted was to follow in her mom's footsteps to become the most powerful and feared sorceress in Auradon, to someone who uses her abilities to help others regardless of what she'll get in return. Mom taught me to look out only for myself, but this year friends new and old have taught me the lesson that I'm never alone—they'll always be there for me, and I'll be there for them. Despite all her scheming and power, it was the one thing Mom didn't expect—the one thing she never understood...FRIENDSHIP.

—Mal

Family Day Photos

I'll never get that image out of my head of our parents trying to use a computer. —Mal

Come on, guys—deep down you know they missed us!
—Jay

It was kind of nice to see them after so long, though. -Evie

Define "nice"... —Carlos

We look so great here! —Audrey

I always look great. –Chad

Now, if you could just work on your humility...

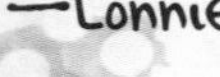

—Lonnie

Croquet is actually pretty fun. —Jay

No kidding! And I actually beat you, for once! —carlos

Did not! —Jay

Did too! —carlos

But you cheated! —Jay

So did you! —carlos

Still wish Mom would use real magic! —Jane

Coronation Day Memories

Thank you for making my big day so memorable! —Ben

I'll never forget your big day, Be
It was life-changing for me! —M

Someday I'll invite you all to my own coronation.—Evie

'll go as long
as there's cake!
—Chad

I wouldn't be caught dead! —Audrey

You may want to trim that list a bit, Evie. —Doug

Not many coronations get crashed by evil dragons.
—Lonnie

hotographic proof that
e wand looks GOOD
n me! —Jane

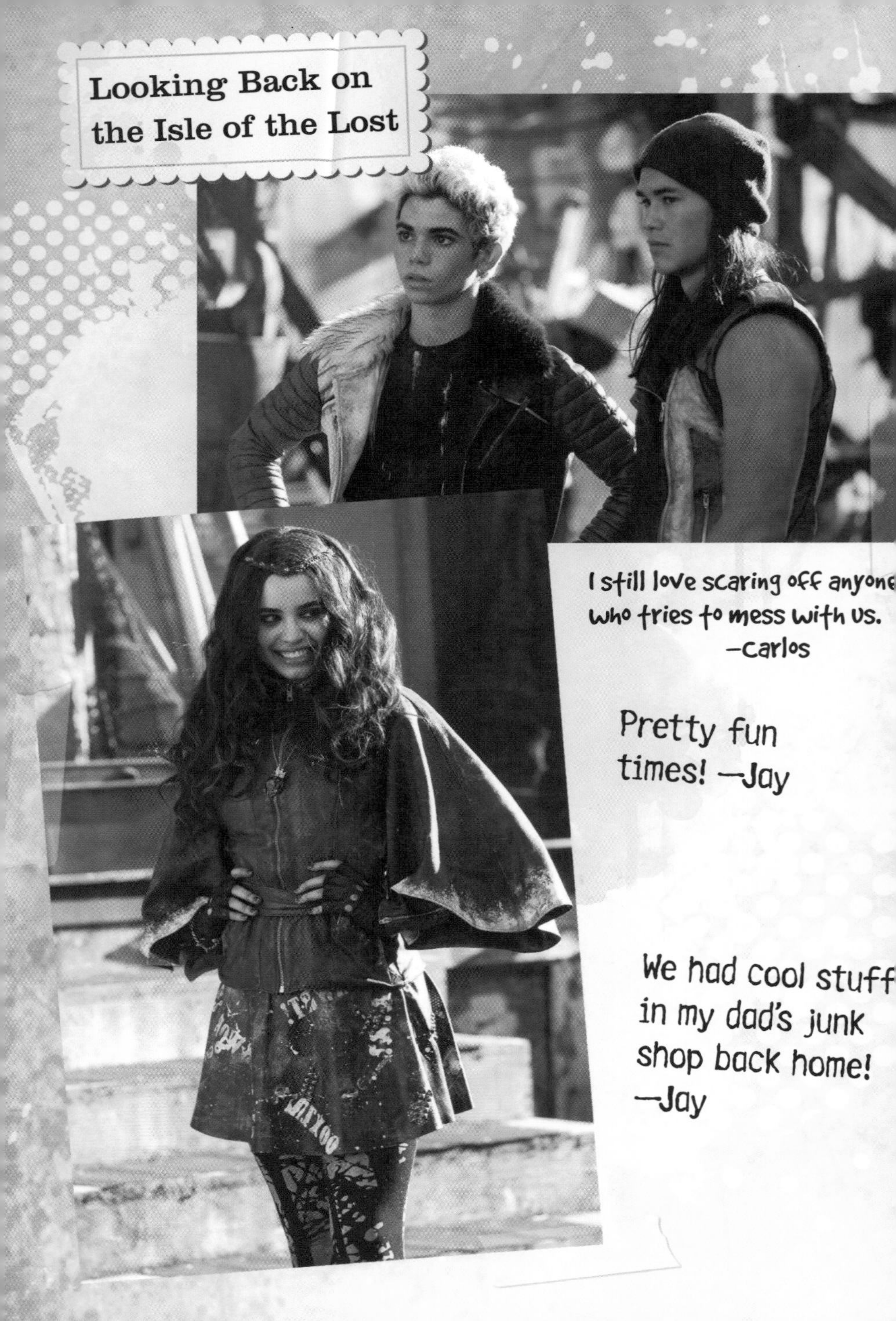
Looking Back on the Isle of the Lost
I still love scaring off anyone who tries to mess with us. –Carlos
Pretty fun times! —Jay
We had cool stuff in my dad's junk shop back home! —Jay

Our old school, Dragon Hall, has got nothing on Auradon Prep! —Mal

Did anyone ever find out what was actually in the Mystery Stew? –Carlos

Remember that adventure at the Forbidden Fortress?

–Evie

How could I forget? I was under that sleep curse for days! —Mal

We'll keep making new memories in Auradon.

–Evie

We'll never forget where we came from—but where we're going is full of new adventures! —Mal

Thanks, all, for the best year ever! —Ben

Stay ROTTEN! —Mal

Mirror, mirror in my hand—hope everyone has the best summer in the land! -Evie

KIT, everyone! —Lonnie

Can't wait for summer school! —Doug

Who's keeping this over the summer? —Audrey

Congratulations to everyone—this year's spirit book is one of the best in the history of Auradon Prep! With so many great contributions, it was difficult to choose just one winner. So there isn't one winner. Instead, you're all winners!

Bibbidi-Bobbidi-Boo!

Fairy Godmother

Time to relax poolside 'til next semester. —Jay

Can we all hang out soon? —Jane

Party at my place! And you're all invited (even you, Mal)! —Audrey

Keep it real! –Chad

I'll take good care of Dude over break. —carlos

OUR BEST CANDY DISCOVERIES

Dwarf Gems

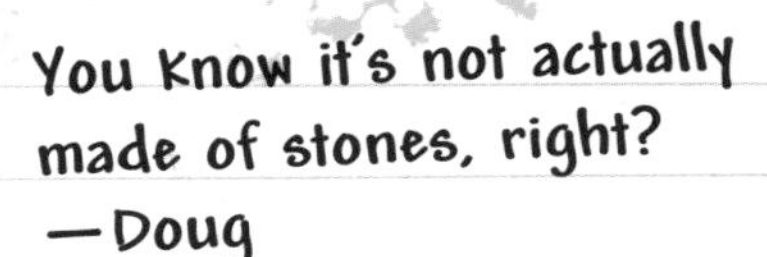

I don't know what cave they mine this stuff from, but I wanna go lick the walls. —Carlos

You know it's not actually made of stones, right? —Doug

That doesn't make sense. Why would they call it GEM candy? —Carlos

Gummi Snakes

Stretchy, sticky, and sweet! —Carlos

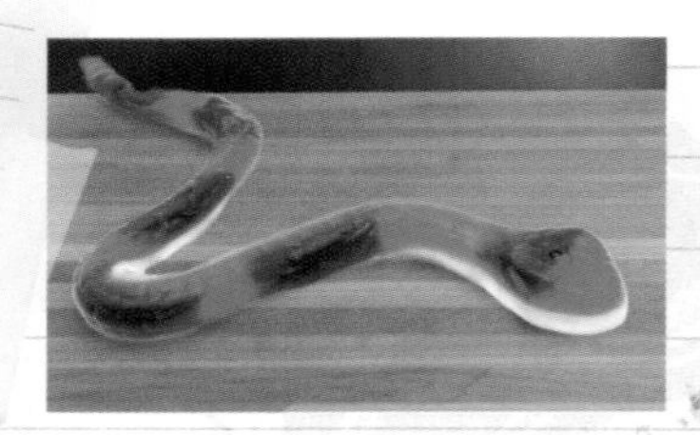

Chocolate

The absolutely, positively BEST thing I've ever tasted! —Carlos

Villain Straps

Taste so sour they'll make your lips pucker. —Carlos

These are my faves! —Mal

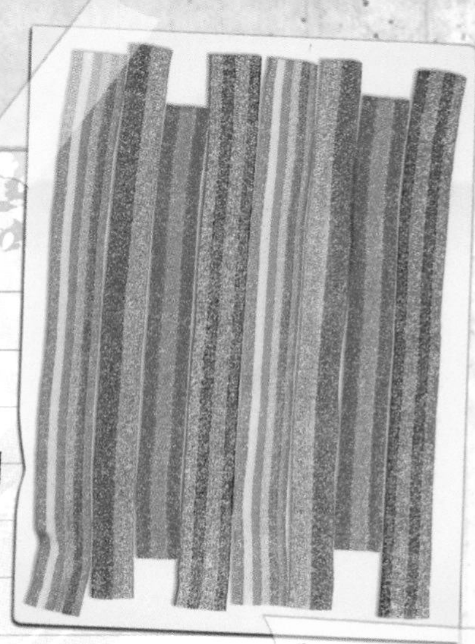

Fairy Bubble Gum

Chew this and you can blow bubbles that float into the air. —Carlos

Just don't blow 'em too big or they can get stuck in your hair. The cheerleading squad had problems a few years ago... —Audrey

Poison Apples

1/3 fruit + 1/3 nuts + 1/3 caramel = 100% tasty! —Carlos

Candy and apples? Now we're talking! —Evie

Things You'd Never Ever Do:

Kiss a frog—prince or not! —Mal

Wear pink. EWW!—Evie

Steal from the needy. —Jay

Hurt Dude (or ANY dog). —Carlos

Misuse my royalty or treat someone unfairly. —Ben

Make someone feel bad about himself or herself. —Lonnie

Turn mice into horses! (Poor things...) —Jane

Curse an entire kingdom because I wasn't invited to a party. —Audrey

Extra credit. —Chad

Play Tourney! —Doug

Some Facts People Probably Don't Know About You:

I told my first lie when I was three. Mom was so proud! —Mal

It usually takes me two hours to get ready in the morning. —Evie

Tigers are my favorite animal. —Jay

I accidentally used Dude's dog shampoo once. My hair's never felt softer. —Carlos

Dad once grounded me for a month for cutting up his favorite rosebush. —Ben

My favorite ice-cream flavor is green tea. —Lonnie

I prefer black licorice over red. —Jane

I have five alarm clock settings because I usually sleep through the first four. —Audrey

Mom's mice really creep me out. -Chad

I'm the tallest person in my family. —Doug

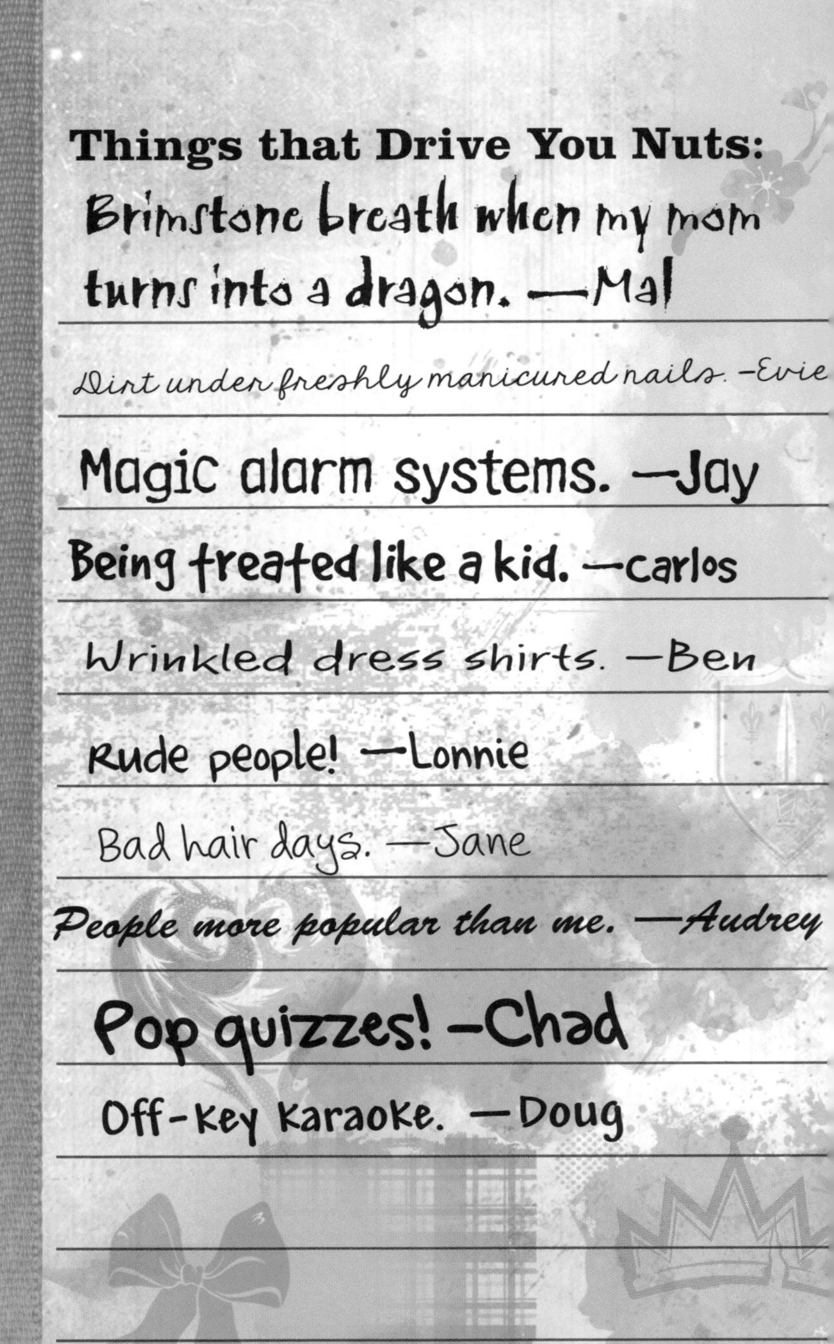

Things that Drive You Nuts:

Brimstone breath when my mom turns into a dragon. —Mal

Dirt under freshly manicured nails. –Evie

Magic alarm systems. —Jay

Being treated like a kid. —Carlos

Wrinkled dress shirts. —Ben

Rude people! —Lonnie

Bad hair days. —Jane

People more popular than me. —Audrey

Pop quizzes! –Chad

Off-Key Karaoke. —Doug

What Are <u>Your</u> Likes And Dislikes?:

Writer: Andrew Scheppmann
Editor: Amy Nathanson Heaslip
Designer: Rebecca A. Stone
Copy Editor: Mary Bronzini-Klein
Managing Editor: Christine Guido
Creative Director: Julia Sabbagh
Associate Publisher: Rosanne McManus
Disney Team: Chelsea Alon,
Carin R. Davis, Eric Geron,
Rich Thomas, Erin Zimring

Illustrations on pages 21 (dogs), 40 (Tourney Field diagram), 47 (spinning wheel),
and 57 (dragons and castle) by Andrew Barthelmes

ISBN 978-0-7944-3772-5
Published by Studio Fun International, Inc.
44 South Broadway, White Plains, NY 10601 U.S.A. and
Studio Fun International Limited,
The Ice House, 124-126 Walcot Street, Bath UK BA1 5BG

Printed in China.
10 9 8 7 6 5 4 3 2 1
SL2/04/16

AURADON PREP
Power of Good
Born to Rule
Be Yourself